# ACROSS THE SEA

By Ruth Homberg

Based on the original story by Brittany Candau

Illustrated by the Disney Storybook Art Team

Random House 🏠 New York

Elsa and Anna are going
on a trip!
They will set sail
to see new places.

# Dear Parents:

Congratulations! Your child is taking
the first steps on an exciting journey.
The destination? Independent reading!

**STEP INTO READING®** will help ̲ ̲ ̲hild get there. The program offers
five steps to reading success. Ea ̲ ̲ ̲ ̲ ̲ ̲ ̲s fun stories ̲ ̲ ̲ ̲olorful
art or photographs. In addition ̲ ̲ ̲ ̲ ̲nd
characters, there are Step into R ̲ ̲ ̲ ̲ ̲ Re ̲
and Boxed Sets, Sticker Reader ̲ ̲ ̲ ̲ ̲ ̲ rs—
program with something to int ̲ ̲ ̲ ̲

## Learning to Rea ̲ ̲ ̲ ̲ ̲p!

### Ready to Re ̲ ̲ ̲ ̲l–Kinderg ̲ ̲ ̲n
• big type and ea ̲ ̲ ̲ ne and rhythm • picture c ̲ ̲
For children wh ̲ ̲ ̲ ̲e alphabet and are eager to
begin reading.

### Reading with Help ̲ ̲ ̲ ̲ –Grade 1
• basic vocabulary • sho ̲ ̲ ̲ ̲simple stories
For children who recog ̲ ̲ ̲ ̲ words and sound o ̲
new words with help.

### Reading on Your Own    Grades 1–3
• en ̲ ̲ ̲ ̲ ̲haracters • easy-to-follow plots • popular topics
F ̲ ̲ ̲ ̲who are ready to rea ̲ ̲ ̲ ̲ own.

### R ̲ ̲ ̲ ̲agraphs
• ̲ ̲ ̲ ̲ ̲ vocabulary ̲ ̲ ̲ ̲ ̲citing stories
For newly independen ̲ ̲ ̲ ̲ ̲ ̲ple sentences
with confidence.

### Ready for Chapters
• chapters • longer paragraphs ̲ ̲
For children who want to take the pl ̲ ̲ ̲ ̲ ̲er books
but still like colorful pictures.

**STEP INTO READING®** is designed to give every child a successful
reading experience. The grade levels are only guides; children will progress
through the steps at their own speed, developing confidence in their reading.

Remember, a lifetime love of reading starts with a single step!

Step into Reading, Random House, and the Random House colophon are registered trademarks of Penguin Random House LLC.

Visit us on the Web!
StepIntoReading.com
randomhousekids.com

Educators and librarians, for a variety of teaching tools, visit us at RHTeachersLibrarians.com

ISBN 978-0-7364-3398-3 (trade) — ISBN 978-0-7364-8215-8 (lib. bdg.)
ISBN 978-0-7364-3399-0 (ebook)

Printed in the United States of America   10 9 8 7 6

Elsa packs.

Anna looks

out the window.

The ship is ready!

Anna steers the ship.
Elsa looks
at the map.

Elsa uses her magic.

She makes a strong wind

to fill the sails.

Land ho!

Soon they arrive
in a new kingdom.
Elsa and Anna meet
the king and queen.

They try new foods.

They see new kinds

of flowers.

The king and queen
throw a party
for Anna and Elsa.

Anna learns
a new dance.

Anna and Elsa
visit another kingdom.
Elsa sees art
with the queen.

Anna plays
with a funny animal!

The queen shows Elsa

a block of ice.

She asks Elsa

to carve

an ice sculpture.

Will Elsa use her magi

Elsa is too shy.

Anna carves a snowman

in the ice.

It looks like Olaf!

Anna and Elsa
visit another city.
They see the Duke!

The city is very hot.
The Duke does not
like the heat.

Anna and Elsa walk
with the Duke.
Everyone in the city
is hot and sticky.

Elsa wants to help.

She uses her magic.

It starts to snow!

The people cheer!

Elsa makes

frosty drinks.

Everyone feels better.

Even the Duke is happy.

Anna and Elsa

ride sleds.

People ice-skate.

Anna is proud of Elsa.
She sprays the Duke
with snow!
*Brrr!*

It is time to sail home.
Anna and Elsa wave
goodbye to their
new friends.
They had such a fun trip
across the sea!